The
WAITING PLACE

Written and Illustrated by Marc Sutherland

H A R R Y   N .   A B R A M S ,   I N C . ,   P U B L I S H E R S

Sometimes I just can't sleep.

Maybe it's because my toes itch,
And the rickety floorboards creak,
While along in the bath the faucet drips,
And the rusty old bedsprings squeak.

Maybe it's Old Man Apple Tree
Reaching through my window,
While timberwolves sing moon songs
To the deep, dark shadows below.

It's hard to wait in pajamas
For a shiny, clear morning to come,
When that bedroom door is wide open,
With many great things to be done.

But tomorrow I'll grow pumpkins,
The biggest in the state.
They'll haunt each Halloween doorstep
And be pie on everyone's plate.

I'll ramble with the animals
And ask the willing ones
To sing me lazy lullabies
Beneath the setting sun.

I'll march with soldiers of the Queen,
Who've come from far away.
We'll step off to the bass drum beat
To celebrate the day.

11

I'll visit with Grandmother Gryphon;
Great games of chess we'll share.
She'll spread her wings to the washing waves,
And we'll savor the salty sea air.

Tucked inside my submarine,
And deep beneath the storm,
I'll look about in oceans old,
Down where it's safe and warm.

Snowshoeing up in frosty North Woods,

Under those snow-filled skies,

I'll ask the tired old Yeti Man

For tea and words that are wise.

Floating along in a longboat,
Laughing on slippery seas,
We'll chase the icy breezes,
Eleven stout Vikings and me.

Guided by starlight and comet dust,
Rising by hot-air balloon,
I'll walk and talk with the astronauts
And dance with the Man in the Moon.

"It's seven o'clock, time to wake up!"

The town is silently sleeping.
The fields are wrapped up in white.
A blizzard blew in with the morning.
I bounce 'round the room in delight.

I'm happy to say there's no school today,
The snow is steadily falling.
My long johns are on, my sled's in the shed,
And the hills are quietly calling.

There's no need to wait any longer,
Tomorrow is here, you see.
All the places I hoped for are waiting,
Just waiting out there for me.

⁓ For Mom, Dad, Sarah, and Tim ⁓

EDITOR: Robert Morton
DESIGNER: Dana Sloan

LIBRARY OF CONGRESS CATALOGING-IN-PUBLICATION DATA
Sutherland, Marc, 1968–
The waiting place / written and illustrated by Marc Sutherland
p.   cm.
Summary: When he has trouble falling asleep, a young boy
imagines all kinds of amazing things going on in his bedroom.
ISBN 0–8109–3994–0 (hardcover)
[Dreams—Fiction. 2. Imagination—Fiction. 3. Stories in rhyme.]
I. Title.
PZ8.3.S968Wai   1998
[E]—dc21   97–39088

Printed and bound in France
Harry N. Abrams, Inc.
100 Fifth Avenue
New York, N.Y. 10011
www.abramsbooks.com